E
RIGGIO, Anita
Beware the Brindlebeast

BEWARE the BRINDLEBEAST

retold & illustrated by ANITA RIGGIO

Boyds Mills Press

BEWARE THE BRINDLEBEAST is retold from "The
Hedley Kow" as found in Joseph Jacobs's *More English
Fairy Tales* (1904) and in Ethel Johnston Phelps's
Tatterhood and Other Tales (Feminist Press, 1978).

Published by Caroline House
Boyds Mills Press, Inc.
A Highlights Company
815 Church Street
Honesdale, Pennsylvania 18431
Printed in Mexico

Publisher Cataloging-in-Publication Data
Riggio, Anita.
     Beware the Brindlebeast / retold and illustrated by
Anita Riggio.—1st ed.
[32]p. : col. ill. ; cm.
Based upon "The Hedley Kow" from Joseph Jacobs's
More English Fairy Tales, 1904.
Summary : Retelling of the English tale about the Dread
Brindlebeast, who has magical powers.
ISBN 1-56397-133-X
1. Folklore—Great Britain—Juvenile literature. [1. Folklore
—Great Britain. 2. Fairy tales.] I. Title.
398.2—dc20   1994   CIP   AC E
Library of Congress Catalog Card Number 93-70875

First edition, 1994
Book designed by Alice Lee Groton
The text of this book is set in 16.5-point Goudy Old Style.
The illustrations are oil paintings.
Distributed by St. Martin's Press

10 9 8 7 6 5 4 3 2 1

For LINDA GABIANELLI,
children's librarian extraordinaire

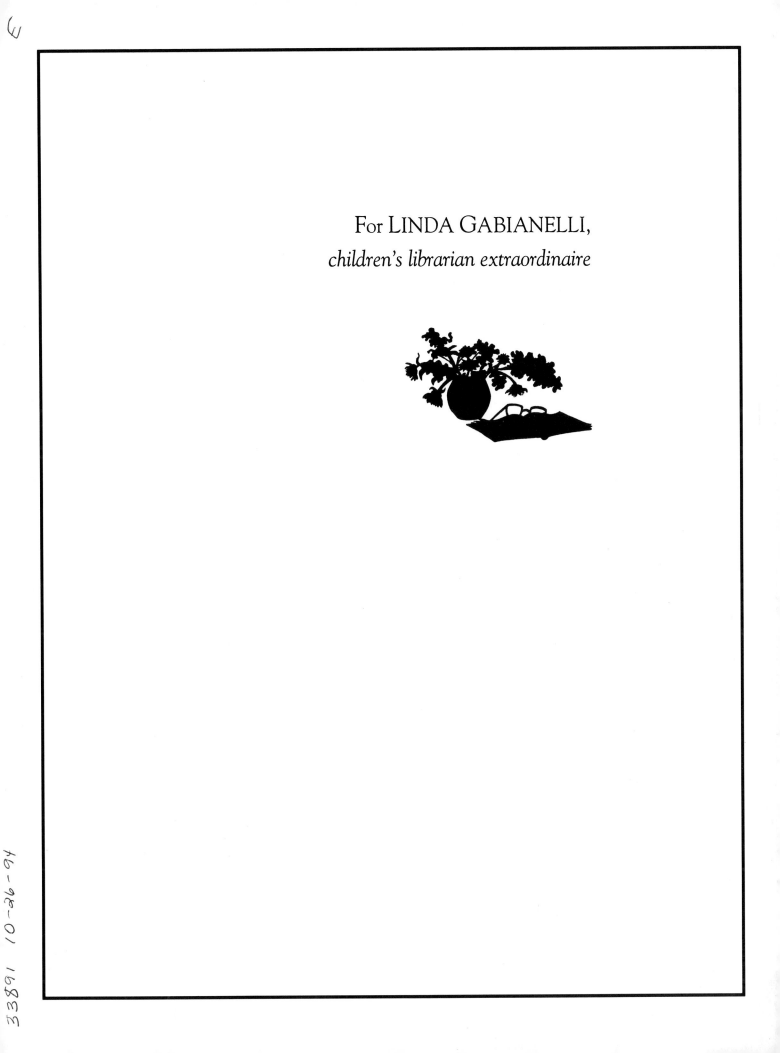

Birdie was a cheerful old woman who lived with her marmalade cat in a bitty cottage just outside the village. She was surely poor but got along one way or another and was glad of it.

To earn a living, Birdie did chores for the housewives in the hamlet. They gave her a meal at noontime, plus a supper of stale bread and hard cheese, and insisted that Birdie begin work at dawn's light so she could be safely home before darkness fell.

For all the villagers were afraid of the Dread Brindlebeast who roamed the village at night, changing itself into frightful forms and scaring the gentle village folk right out of their wits. "Beware the Brindlebeast!" the housewives warned Birdie. Beware, indeed.

Now, it was All Hallows Eve, the very night of lurking goblins and ghosties. The evening star winked at the rows of weathered gravestones as Birdie hastened homeward past the old burying ground.

A black cat darted across her path and vanished into the shadows. Birdie gathered her shawl closer and, looking after the cat, nearly tripped over a great black kettle squatting there smack in the middle of the road.

"Now who could have left this here?" she said, standing over it with her great gnarled hand on her hip. "It's a fine pot, to be sure."

Birdie scanned the field before her and the road behind, but not a soul did she see.

She shifted her basket. "It's likely to have a hole, I suppose. Still, it would make a handsome tub for my blue asters. Maybe I'll help myself to it anyway." And with that thought she crouched down, knees creaking, and lifted the lid to look inside.

"Mercy!" Birdie gasped. "It's full to the brim with gold pieces!" Jaw to chest, Birdie gaped at the gold, wondering at her good luck. Birdie could hardly take her eyes from the treasure. "My, my, my," she mumbled, "how shall I get this kettle home?"

After several moments, Birdie scrambled to her feet and tied one end of her shawl around the pot. Then, step by step, she dragged the kettle homeward, humming as she went.

"My goodness!" she said, interrupting her tune. "Think of the fine home I could have, one with polished wooden floors and patterned rugs, embroidered linens, and the finest china teacups. Why, fancy inviting the village housewives to tea!"

Under the gaze of the gleaming moon, Birdie crossed the narrow footbridge. The dusk crept behind her across the meadow, slipping into snug places, tucking itself into burrows and hollows.

Birdie glanced over her shoulder. "Goodness gracious!" she cried in surprise. "My pot of gold has turned into a barrel of apples!" And so it had.

She stood over the barrel, blinking. "I could have sworn this was a kettle of gold," she said at last, "but that must have been only a lovely dream. Ah well, a stout barrel of apples is still a fine treasure." And with that, Birdie picked up the end of her shawl and set off homeward, dragging the barrel behind her.

"There will be apples enough to make cobblers and pies to share," said Birdie. "And still there will be some left to store in the root cellar over winter. What good luck!"

As Birdie reached the great sycamore at the foot of her own little knoll, night spread like a blanket across the meadow. Birdie wheeled around.

"Now this beats all!" she cried. "Instead of a barrel of apples, here's a fat pumpkin at the end of my shawl!" And so it was.

Then said Birdie, "Well now! A pumpkin is just what I need to make a jack-o'-lantern for All Hallows Eve!" And being ever so anxious to see how it would look, Birdie picked up the pumpkin and bustled up the hill to her tiny cottage. She stepped inside and shut the door.

Outside, the wind began to wail. Whorls of golden leaves skittered across Birdie's yard, over her doorstep, and pat-pat-pattered at her little wooden door.

But Birdie set about carving her pumpkin just the same. "Lucky me," Birdie chuckled, scooping it out. "Such a treasure will make a jolly jack-o'-lantern and lots of pies as well!"

When she had finished, Birdie found a small candle to put inside the jack-o'-lantern and grandly placed the pumpkin on her doorstep. She retrieved a flaming twig from the hearth and touched the flame to the candlewick. When the wick took the flame, Birdie straightened her stiff back.

"There now," Birdie sighed and stood for a moment to admire it.

Nothing stirred. Not a creature, not the wind, not the night.

Suddenly that pumpkin let out a high-pitched squeal. It hopped right off the doorstep and over Birdie!

The jack-o'-lantern throbbed with a ferocious glow. It snorted fire from its nostrils. Flames burst from the top of its head, singeing the pumpkin cap.

"Heavens!" Birdie cried.

Before her astonished eyes, that jack-o'-lantern pitched and puckered and pulsed. The hideous thing swelled and swelled, and when it looked as if it would burst, it shot out four muscled legs, shook out two cropped ears, and brandished a great flaxen tail!

Shrieking something terrible, it reared its gigantic head, fiery eyes blazing in their sockets. And that beast bucked and kicked and thrashed, nearly knocking over the little house right where it stood!

Just then a little smile flickered in Birdie's eyes. Folding her arms across her bosom, she said, "Well, this *is* my lucky day! Fancy me having the Dread Brindlebeast all to myself, with not another soul around to join the fun!"

"FUN!" bellowed the beast. "I do not intend this to be fun! Why, you should be scared out of your wits like the rest of the gentle village folk!"

Birdie sashayed back and forth, a smile dancing in her eyes. "Is that so?" she replied.

"Yes, that's so!" the Brindlebeast wailed. "Most folks fear and curse me and are jolly well frightened to pieces!"

"Well, I am *not!*" said Birdie, poking the beast's belly with a crooked finger. "Why, goodness gracious, your company made my walk home so much more exciting. Besides, there's no harm done. Look here. I still have a bit of cheese and bread for my supper. So, thank you, Brindlebeast. And good eve to you."

With that, Birdie gathered her shawl about her shoulders and stepped right past the Brindlebeast to her own little door and went inside.

But turning back to eye the beast one last time, she saw not a beast but a little fellow shuffling his feet on Birdie's doorstep.

"Ho!" Birdie started. "Nothing more than spit and fire and smoke, was it?" Then she let out a great sigh. "Well now, would you care to share some supper?"

"Don't mind if I do," the Brindlebeast answered.

So they sat down to supper, and somehow that bitty wedge of cheese grew to six times its size. In a twinkling there appeared some nicely boiled brown eggs and several biscuits for their tea.

They made a cheerful meal of it, and when they had finished, they sat by Birdie's cozy fire.

Then Birdie listened to the Brindlebeast's tales until her sides ached with laughter and tears rolled down her plump cheeks. "I don't know when an evening's been so quickly spent," she said, dabbing her eyes with a hankie.

Over time the little fellow came often for a bit of supper and chats by the fire. And when Birdie found her woodpile stacked as high as the roof and her cupboard stocked with biscuits and cheese aplenty, she very wisely said nothing about it to anyone.

The gentle village folk still spoke in terrified tones of the Dread Brindlebeast, but Birdie never let on, save for the little smile that flickered in her eyes.